THE PREHISTORIC GAMES

Janet Lawler ✻ Illustrated by Martin Davey

PELICAN PUBLISHING COMPANY
GRETNA 2016

ISBN 9781455621385
E-book ISBN 9781455621392

Printed in Malaysia

Published by Pelican Publishing Company, Inc.
1000 Burmaster Street, Gretna, Louisiana 70053

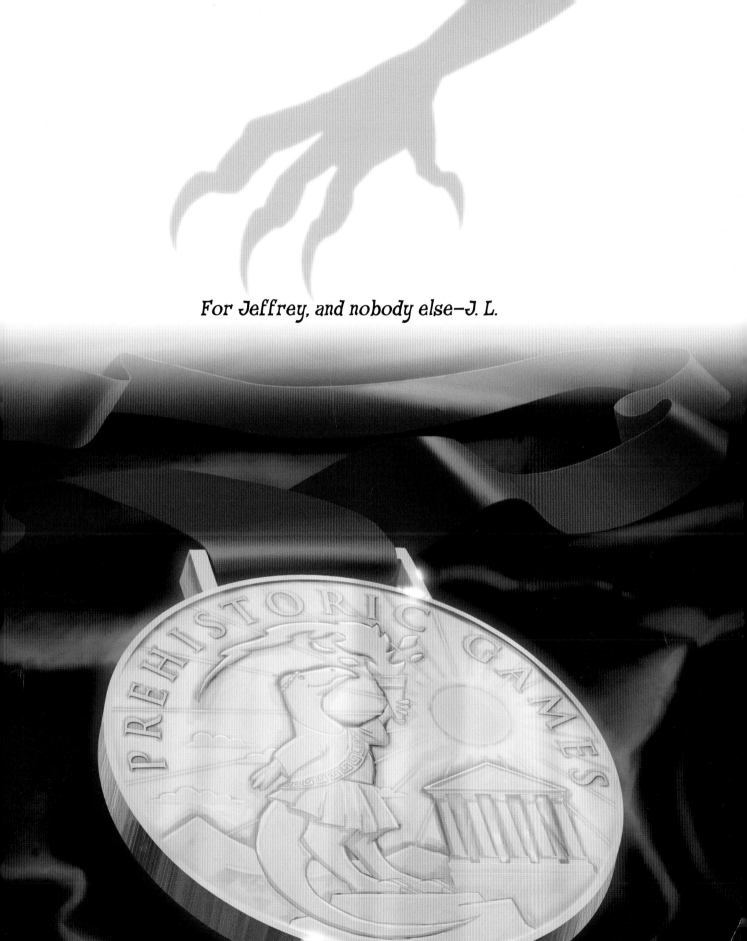

For Jeffrey, and nobody else—J. L.

They happen every thousand years—
the Prehistoric Games.
To start things off, a torch is lit
by hot volcanic flames.

The dinosaurs parade in rows.
They're ready, fit, and trim
from years of heavy training
in the fields and jungle gym.

Participants are warming up
as nighttime fades to dawn,
eager to compete in sports
to show off speed or brawn.

T. Rex is prone and puffing hard,
with arms too short and weak.
Raptors dash around the track,
racing cheek to cheek.

Triceratops face off in pairs
to wrestle on a mat,
employing special three-horned holds
to pin opponents flat.

Teenage allosaurs pump up
with sets of barbell curls,
hoping two-ton weights impress
the judges and the girls.

Gymnastic competition starts.
Troodons run and thud.
They spring into each vault and stick
their landings in the mud.

Officials use their teeth or tails
to hold the scorecards high,
while waiting athletes chew their claws.
Some cheer and others cry.

The maiasauras elevate
in tumbling floor routines,
before attempting somersaults
on springy trampolines.

Pteranodon, with wings outspread,
can loop the highest bar.
Crowds adore the dismount
of this fine gymnastic star.

The Prehistoric Games fly by
until the final day,
when team events take place before
a trial sport display.

Stegosaurs play volleyball.
They leap and lunge and crash.

Coconuts are kept aloft
as setups for a smash.

Then demonstration dodgeball starts
and tension quickly grows,

as herbivores and carnivores
create two separate rows.

The action's fierce; the bellows loud.
They're trading knockout hits.
Every time a throw connects,
another player sits.

At sunset, only two still stand;
the referee is heard,
declaring that the game is tied—
she has the final word.

Contestants join the closing march
and gather one last time,
to celebrate a special week
of athletes in their prime.

Apatosaur accepts a medal,
forged in lava flows,
for fostering good sportsmanship
and making friends of foes.

The dinosaurs exchange high-fives
and shed gigantic tears—
for now the Games are over
for another thousand years.

GLOSSARY

barbell: a metal bar with weights on each end, used in weightlifting

brawn: strength; big, strong muscles

carnivore: a meat-eating animal

foster: to encourage; to help grow or develop

herbivore: a plant-eating animal

lava flow: a stream of extremely hot liquid rock that pours out from an active volcano

somersault: a forward or backward full roll of the body on the ground or in the air

vault: a leap or large jump, often started by running and using hands to push

PRONUNCIATION GUIDE

allosaur: AL-uh-sor

apatosaur: uh-PAT-uh-sor

maiasaura: my-uh-SOR-uh

pteranodon: ter-AN-uh-don (ignore the *p!*)

stegosaur: STEG-uh-sor

triceratops: try-SAIR-uh-tops

troodon: TROH-uh-don